William and the Guinea-pig

First published 2001 by
A & C Black (Publishers) Ltd
37 Soho Square
London WID 3QZ

Text copyright © Citizenship Foundation 2001
Illustrations copyright © Tim Archbold 2001

The rights of Gill Rose and Tim Archbold to be
identified as author and illustrator of this work
have been asserted by them in accordance with
the Copyrights, Designs and Patents Act 1988.

ISBN 0-7136-5837-1

A CIP catalogue for this book is available from
the British Library.

Published in conjunction with the
Citizenship Foundation.
Sponsored by British Telecom.

Printed in Malta on behalf of
Midas printing (UK) Ltd.

William and the Guinea-pig

by Gill Rose

Illustrated by Tim Archbold

The school had a new guinea-pig.
William was thrilled when he was
allowed to hold him.

Soon it would
be his birthday.

"Please, please can I have
a guinea-pig of my own?"
he begged his mum.

"I'm sorry," said Mum, "but I won't have time to look after a guinea-pig as well as working all day at the shop."

"I'll look after it all by myself," promised William.
"You won't have to do anything."

"Well, all right then," said Mum.

When William woke up on his birthday,
he was very excited.

Mum led him to the garden shed
with Kelly, his little sister.
William saw the brand-new hutch
and rushed over to open the door.

There, sitting on a pile of straw,
was the most beautiful
golden-haired guinea-pig.

6

"He's fantastic!" shouted William.
"I'm going to call him Sandy."

"Can I hold him please, William?"
asked Kelly.

"No," said William.
"He's mine and you're too young."

7

For the first few days, William spent most of his spare time down in the shed looking after Sandy.

He even forgot about playing football with Rafiq, his best friend.

Every day, Kelly asked William
if she could help, but William
always said no.

"That's not fair," said Kelly.

"It's William's guinea-pig,"
Mum said.
"If he says you can't help,
then you can't."

Kelly was cross with William for being so horrible.
Sometimes she sneaked into the shed
when he wasn't there, just to look at Sandy.
But she made sure Mum didn't see her.

On Saturday William wanted to play football with
Rafiq. It seemed a long time since their last game.

"You can go when you've cleaned
out Sandy's hutch," Mum said.

"I'll do it later, honest,"
said William.

A few days later William and Kelly's cousin Rachel came to visit.

"Show Rachel your new guinea-pig, William," said Mum.

Suddenly, William began to feel very bad.
It had been days since he had been
to see Sandy. He wondered what happens
to a guinea-pig that has not been fed.

"Can't I show her later?" he said.

"No, let's go now," Mum said,
"before we have our tea."

13

As they walked towards the shed,
William felt his face getting
redder and redder. Mum would
be so angry with him.

"She might take Sandy
away from me," he thought.

But when they opened the door
of the shed, William had a big surprise.

There was Sandy sitting happily in
his nice clean hutch. He had lots of food
in his bowl and his bottle was full of water.

Sandy began to squeak as Kelly poked
some fresh leaves through the wire.
Then William knew who had been
looking after him.

"Well done, William," said Mum, smiling.

"You've been very good."

At bedtime, when Rachel had gone,
William found Kelly reading in bed.

"Thanks, Kelly," he said.
"I'm sorry I said you were too young
to help look after Sandy."

And from then on, they shared their beautiful golden-haired guinea-pig.

William and Kelly agreed that
it was a good idea to help each
other. And Rafiq was happy too.

21

Something to think about...

* Why do you think William wants a pet?

* What do you think a guinea-pig needs for a happy, healthy life?

* What things do people need to keep them alive, healthy and happy? Do you think people need more things than animals to keep them happy?

* Some people think that keeping animals in cages is wrong. Why do you think they think this? Do you agree or disagree?

* Do you think William's mum was wrong to let William have a pet? Why do you think this?

* Was Mum right to trust William when he said he would look after Sandy?

* What does it mean to trust someone?

* How would you describe William's behaviour towards Sandy?

* Was it OK for William not to let Kelly help look after Sandy?

* What could you have said to persuade William to let Kelly help with Sandy?

* When Kelly found out that William wasn't looking after Sandy, she began to do it herself secretly. Do you think that was the right thing to do?

* Kelly could have told her mum that William had forgotten Sandy. Why do you think she didn't do that?

* Do you think Kelly was right not to tell on William?

* People often say that it is wrong to tell tales. Why do they say this? Do you agree? Can you think of times when it might not be wrong?

* William did not own up when Mum said he was looking after Sandy well. What do you think about that?

* Think about what happened when William said sorry. How hard do you think that was for William?

* Why is it hard to say sorry sometimes?

* Kelly forgave William for what he had done. What does it mean to forgive someone? Is it easy to do?

* William and Kelly thought that helping each other look after Sandy was a good idea. Who was it good for, and how?

* Talk about times when working with others may be difficult. What makes it difficult?